CINDY DERBY

# BLURP'S
# Book of
# Manners

Roaring Brook Press
New York

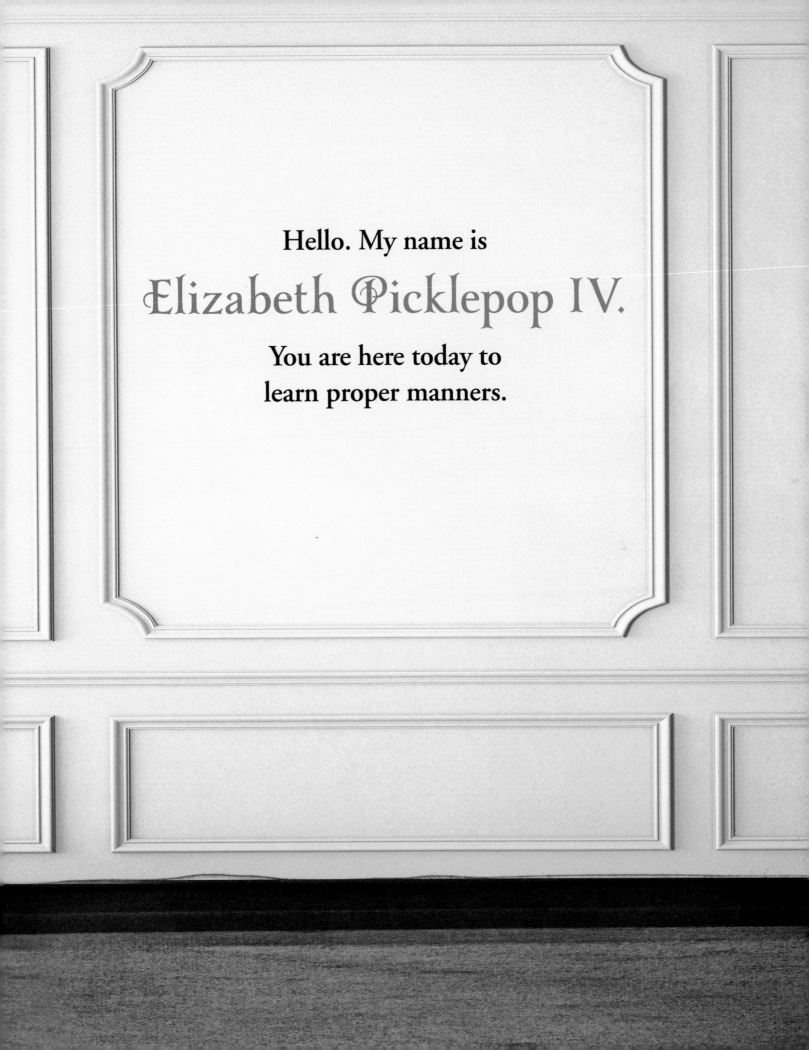

Hello. My name is

# Elizabeth Picklepop IV.

You are here today to
learn proper manners.

Upon finishing this course,
participants will be presented with
a certificate of completion.

I will be watching each and every one
of you VERY closely. So pay attention.

We are going to start with:

# How to Properly Introduce Yourself

Please ignore what just happened. Erase it from your mind, thank you.

Moving forward in our lesson in introducing yourself . . .

First, one must stand up straight.

Look the other person in the eyes.

Smile in a pleasant way, then . . .

Well . . . isn't that peculiar?
Pay no attention to that.
None at all.

For our next lesson, let's gracefully
move outside to the garden.

Everyone, I would like you to meet
Professor Ham and his darling pet, Edgar.

When making pleasant conversation, one must always listen more than they talk.

Professor Ham, how did you come up with your fascinating theory on the Law and Economics of Hamster Wheel?

Oh, would you look at that! Professor Ham . . .
had to go. Moving right along!

# How to Sit Down Properly for Afternoon Tea

Presenting yourself well is the most important goal, no matter where you are.

To sit properly, stand as close as possible to the seat,

put your knees together, ease down into the chair gently, and—

If something should go unplanned . . .
then simply excuse yourself and
proceed with dignity.

Cross your ankles, place your hands like so,

and sit quietly with perfect and poised posture.

To get up from your seat, say "pardon me"

and graciously walk away.

Keep your composure.

Politely lean
into the turn.

BLURP!

BLURP!

BLURP!

BLURP!

BLURP!

BLURP!

BLURP!

BLURP!

BLURP!

BLURP!

BLURP!

BLURP!

BLURP!

BLURP!

# ENOUGH!!!
You are RUINING
everything!

Let's pretend that didn't happen. Please join me for our last, very important lesson . . .

How to Be Considerate

When we are considerate,
people want to be around us!

That is why it is
important to treat
others with warmth . . .

And kindness . . .

I'm sorry.

For Allie, Simone, Tyler, and Maven

Published by Roaring Brook Press
Roaring Brook Press is a division of Holtzbrinck Publishing Holdings Limited Partnership
120 Broadway, New York, NY 10271 • mackids.com

Our books may be purchased in bulk for promotional, educational, or business use.
Please contact your local bookseller or the Macmillan Corporate and Premium Sales Department at (800) 221-7945
ext. 5442 or by email at MacmillanSpecialMarkets@macmillan.com.

Library of Congress Control Number: 2022908284

First edition, 2022
The art in this book was created by collaging pieces of 1950s home decor magazines,
using digital tools, and splattering ink and watercolor from across a room.
This book was edited by Emily Feinberg and
designed by Mariam Quraishi with art direction by Sharismar Rodriguez.
The production was supervised by Allene Cassagnol, and the production editor
was Jacqueline Hornberger. The text was set in Garamond, and the display type is Yana.
Printed in China by RR Donnelley Asia Printing Solutions Ltd., Dongguan City, Guangdong Province

ISBN 978-1-250-81035-9
1 3 5 7 9 10 8 6 4 2